The Talk

Alicia D. Williams

Illustrated by Briana Mukodiri Uchendu

A CAITLYN DLOUHY BOOK

ATHENEUM BOOKS FOR YOUNG READERS

New York London Toronto Sydney New Delhi

ATHENEUM BOOKS FOR YOUNG READERS

An imprint of Simon & Schuster Children's Publishing Division
1230 Avenue of the Americas, New York, New York 10020
Text © 2022 by Alicia D. Williams
Illustration © 2022 by Briana Mukodiri Uchendu
ATHENEUM BOOKS FOR YOUNG READERS is
a registered trademark of Simon & Schuster, Inc.
Atheneum logo is a trademark of Simon & Schuster, Inc.
For information about special discounts for bulk purchases,
please contact Simon & Schuster Special Sales at
1-866-506-1949 or business@simonandschuster.com.
The Simon & Schuster Speakers Bureau can bring authors
to your live event. For more information or to book an
event, contact the Simon & Schuster Speakers Bureau at
1-866-248-3049 or visit our website at
www.simonspeakers.com.
The text for this book was set in Coop.
The illustrations for this book were rendered digitally.
Manufactured in China
0622 SCP
First Edition
10 9 8 7 6 5 4 3 2 1
CIP data for this book is available from the Library of
Congress.
ISBN 9781534495296
ISBN 9781534495302 (eBook)

For Cuauthy. One of the funniest, cutest, curious, and bravest boys I know.
—A. W.

To my family—Alexus, Bianca, Alyssa, E.J., Mom, and Dad.
—B. M. U.

Hi, I'm Jay.

These are my friends,

Jamal, Eboni, and Bryant.

Most Saturdays, we race down our block and back like track stars.

See my high tops? They help me run super-duper fast.

We lose track of who wins the most.

But I think I'm the fastest.

This is my grandpa. He cheers us on.

When we stop to rest, he tells us stories about Olympic heroes like

John Carlos,

Wilma Rudolph,

and Jesse Owens.

See this wall?

Here, Mom measures my height.
She makes one teensy tiny mark.

Geesh, not even an inch.
I'm NEVERRR going to grow!

Look at my cheeks.
Nana says they're chubby.

She squeezes them every chance she gets.
I whine and groan that I don't like it.
(But shhh, really, I do.)

Wanna see my wallet?

It's got my favorite superhero on it, see?
I'm strong like him too.
When I grow up, I'm going to
have huge muscles.

I saved a whole five dollars, too!

I earned it doing chores.
Mom says I'm a good
bed-maker-upper.

And when Mom takes me to the store, I buy whatever I want.

Oh, this is our car.

Daddy lets me sit behind the wheel.
He says, *One day this'll be yours.*
I pretend to drive. Vroom! I can't wait!

I ask Mom to measure me at the wall again,
and she says, *Boy, you've grown!*

And I say, *But my feet still don't reach
the gas pedal.*

You like my jacket?

It has a wolf on the back, see?

The hood is soft, too.

It blocks the wind from howling in my ears.

Now look at our wall.
Two whole inches!

I say, *No one can call me*
shrimp anymore.

Mom looks sad.

She says, *They won't see you as a young boy anymore, either.*

I tell her I'll always be her little man.

Remember my friends?

Bryant says,
We're best friends for life.

Jamal says,
Yeah, forever like infinity.

Eboni says,
*We're tighter
than the lid
on a pickle jar.*

We are.

We skateboard up the street and back.

Then we debate whose flips are the best.

There's my storytelling grandpa
watching us laugh and
goof around like usual.

But today, instead of telling us a story, Grandpa does something strange.

He warns us not to crowd in groups of four or more.

Grandpa says, *I believe y'all could be the next Thurgood Marshall, Elijah McCoy, and Bessie Coleman.*

But some folks might think you're the next troublemaker.

We don't understand. We're only hanging out.

But Grandpa says, *That don't matter.*

See my face?

Nana says the chub in my cheeks has flattened out. Nothing to squeeze.

I say, *I'm still cute.*

She says, *Baby, I wish everybody would always see you as the cutie you are.*

Nana plants kisses
on my forehead.

I sigh and moan and act as
if I'm too old for that.
(Shh, I'm not too old.)

Guess what?

Dad got me a new wallet.

He says it's 'cause I'm turning into
a responsible young man. It's almost like his, see?
It holds money I earned from raking leaves.
I'm good at it, too.

And, because Mom's wall marking can't keep up with how fast I'm growing, she takes me to the mall for a new hoodie. Before we go in, she lowers her voice and warns, *No playing, no loud talking, and don't put your hands in your pockets unless you're in an open space.*

But what did I do wrong?

Our new car is black. It's slicker than the old one.
As Dad drives, I picture my toes pushing the gas
as we glide down the road. He tells me to listen up.
Listen up means pay attention.

Son, if you're stopped by the police,
keep your hands on the steering wheel
or on the dashboard, and be very, very calm.

Dad doesn't need to worry.
I'll be the safest driver ever.

Check out my new hoodie.

It has Dad's college's name
right on the front, see?

My hoodie makes me feel safe.

I plug earbuds into my ears, cover my head, nod to the beat, open the door to meet my friends, and—

Son!
Hold on!
Wait a second.

This is our living room.

Here's the sofa and the chairs

that Nana, Grandpa, Mom, Dad, and I sit on.

They say,
Jay, it's time we had a talk.

These are the arms that hug me close.

The family that reassures me that I've done nothing wrong,
and no, I'm not to blame.

The eyes that say I'm the beat of their hearts;
the joy in their smiles;
and their brave, beautiful child.

This is me and my friends.

We want to hang and run,
joke and laugh . . .

race and soar,
skate and flip,
be chill and wild . . .

and just be . . .
us.